My Sloppy Tiger Goes to School

Story by Joy Cowley

It was a mistake
to take my sloppy tiger
to school.

When he saw the computer,
he got very excited.
He bounded over to it
and hit all the keys at once.

"Computers are not for tigers,"
said the teacher.

4

My sloppy tiger
thought the teacher was nice.
He jumped up and licked her face.
"He's tasting me!" said the teacher.

"No," I said. "That's a kiss."

My sloppy tiger loves books.
He doesn't read them.
He eats them.

He tore the books with his claws
and stuffed them in his mouth.

The teacher and I
put the books on the top shelf
where my sloppy tiger
couldn't get them.

He made a fuss
and pretended he was crying.

"Books are not for tigers,"
said the teacher.

My tiger wanted to paint,
but he was too sloppy.
He got paint on the floor.
Then he walked in it.

There were paw prints
all over the classroom.

"Paint is not for tigers!"
we said.

We tried to put on a play.
My sloppy tiger got excited.
He wanted to act all the parts.

When we were singing,
he made a terrible noise.
Singing is definitely not for tigers.

Then recess came.
My sloppy tiger bounded outside.
He ran up and down the playground,
having races with us.

He was very pleased with himself
because he always won.

I think playgrounds
are good for tigers.